The Walker Boys

Adventure Series Book 1

Treasure Hunters

BY JESS WALKER

ILLUSTRATED BY PRADIPTA MUKHERJEE

DEDICATION

This book is affectionately dedicated to my
mother, whose interest in this and all
my other books, was never
less than my own.

CONTENTS

The Game

L ook out! someone yelled.

Max Walker turned his head just in time to see Lorenzo Duke, the meanest bully in Whitebush, charging at him. Two-hundred pounds of muscle flew past him in a rush of air as he dodged the hit. He flung the football downfield to number 72 and hit him right between the numbers. Morgan Walker, Max's younger brother by only a year, spun off a defender and straight-armed another before he sprinted to the end zone.

1

Touchdown!" yelled Morgan as he spiked the football on the ground. A sea of white jerseys swarmed around him in celebration. The whistle blew, and the final score was Whitebush 10, Langville 7.

Max ran over and gave Morgan a high five.

"Another victory!" he shouted.

"Let's go get some refreshments!" someone yelled.

The team headed to the sidelines, led by Marshall Walker, the youngest of the three Walker Boys, who was doing his best rendition of the Wolverine Celebration Dance in front of the cheering crowd.

"Go Marshall, go Marshall, go Marshall!" the crowd chanted as he performed the Wolverine swipe, growl, and crawl.

Marshall loved to dance and always wanted to be the center of attention.

Morgan interrupted the fun. "Hey, guys, don't look now, but trouble is coming."

Max and Marshall glanced over their shoulders and frowned when they saw who it was.

Lorenzo Duke, the meanest bully in Whitebush, approached them with a scowl on his face. He was always getting in trouble at Whitebush Elementary School for picking fights and stealing lunches. He was the same age as Max but stood four inches taller than him.

"What do you want, Lorenzo?" asked Max.

"You got lucky! I should have tackled you. You won't be as lucky next time. Watch your back!" growled Lorenzo.

Marshall nicknamed 'The Bruiser' by his brothers, stepped in front of Max to face the bully.

Lorenzo laughed. "What do you want, little man?"

"You got a bone to pick with my brother, you got a bone to pick with me!"

Morgan rolled his eyes, "Great, Marshall is being Marshall again. What will I have to do this time to keep the peace?"

"You got a lot of bark and no bite, little ma…"

Before Lorenzo could finish, Marshall shoved him to the ground.

Coach Rogers stepped in. "All right, all right, break it up! Nothing to see here! Get going, all of you, before I call your parents!"

The Walker Boys left, leaving an embarrassed Lorenzo Duke sitting on the ground behind them.

Coach Rogers caught up with them. He wanted to have a word with Marshall. "You got a temper on you, son. You better think before you act next time, especially against Lorenzo Duke. If this happens again, I'll bench you for the remainder of the season. Do I make myself clear?"

Marshall nodded his head with a sheepish smile. "Won't happen again, Coach."

"Don't worry, Coach, we'll keep The Bruiser under control," Max and Morgan said.

"Good game, Walkers!" shouted Jerry as he jogged over.

He was one of the Walker Boys' best friends and never missed a game to cheer them on. He was tall and lanky, and skinny as a toothpick, with arms that drooped by his side when he walked.

"Your game ball is on the sidelines with the cheerleaders. Your girlfriend, Missy, is holding onto it for you."

Max shook his head "She's not my girlfriend."

Morgan grinned, "Not what I've heard."

"Max has a girlfriend, Max has a girlfriend," sang Marshall.

Jerry laughed. "Look who's talking, Marshall. My little sister Janie says the two of you are going out."

Marshall blushed and stopped singing. "You're just making that up."

"Say what you will, but I know the facts."

Max looked over and saw the game ball on the ground next to Missy. She waved at him to come over.

"Shall we get the game ball?" asked Max.

"Will I get to hang it up in my bedroom?" teased Jerry.

Morgan slapped him on the shoulder, "Just take a picture of it and hang it on your wall."

"You're full of jokes today, aren't you?" replied Jerry. "I'll see you around, Walker Boys. I have to go and find Janie. I think she's playing with our school mascot, Willy the Wolverine."

They headed over to get the game ball but were only a couple of steps away when it was stolen!

Bullies

Bullies can come in different shapes and sizes. They don't all look the same, and it's not always the biggest or meanest kid whose face is set in a permanent scowl. It can be anyone!

How should you deal with a bully? **WITS**.

- ☑ Walk away
- ☑ Ignore
- ☑ Tell someone
- ☑ Seek help

If this doesn't work, stick up for yourself! You don't want to be a bully's doormat for the rest of your junior school career!

Should Marshall have pushed Lorenzo Duke? No!

Choose words over your fists when dealing with a bully. If all else fails and you must defend yourself, take a page from Marshall's book!

The Treasure Map

It was a dog, and he was fast! In the blink of an eye, the game ball was gone along with the dog into the woods. An older man holding an empty leash ran past.

"He's got the game ball!" shouted Max.

"Stop that dog!" shouted Morgan.

The Walker Boys joined the chase and soon caught up to the white-haired man.

"Please help me get my dog back," he pleaded.

"Don't worry, sir. We'll get your dog back!" said Max, as all three of them ran past.

"Forget the dog, get the ball!" muttered Marshall.

They saw black and white flashes of the dog up ahead, weaving through a blanket of trees.

They saw black and white flashes of the dog up ahead, weaving through a blanket of trees.

"If this dog runs any longer, I'm going to have to buy myself a new pair of shoes," complained Morgan. "The soles are just about worn off!"

Marshall slowed down. "I think he just stopped."

"He's stopped, all right," said Max. "And it looks like he's enjoying our game ball."

"Chewing it up like a bone," echoed Marshall.

Out of breath and their legs ready to fall off, they came to a stop a couple of feet away. Morgan approached the dog. "You guys wait here, I'll get the ball."

When he was close enough, he held out his hand so the dog could sniff it. The dog wagged it's tail and burrowed it's wet nose into Morgan's hand.

"That a boy!" whispered Morgan, as he grabbed hold of the dog's collar.

The white-haired man finally caught up. "There you are, Baxter! Hi, I'm Mr. Barber. I hope Baxter didn't scratch up your ball too badly. Thank you for getting him."

He shook Morgan's hand and waved at Max and Marshall as he took the leash and dragged Baxter away. "I'll remember your kind deed... and by the way, that was one heck of a catch you made."

Morgan blushed. "Thanks."

"Yeah, and don't forget to thank your dog for getting slobber all over the game ball and scratching it up," muttered Marshall.

Max gave him a dirty look. He knew Marshall wasn't one to hold his words back, and this time was no different. Their friend Jerry was just as bad, if not worse. When you got the two of them together, trouble was bound to happen.

Morgan plopped down on the ground. "I'm dog-tired. No pun intended."

Max and Marshall sat next to him.

Max held up the game ball and examined it. "Besides the dog slobber and the teeth marks, it's still in one piece."

He tossed it at Morgan. "Catch."

Morgan felt the dog slobber spray onto his face as he caught it. Max tried hard to suppress a smile.

"Okay, that was gross," Morgan complained, flinging it back at Max.

The ball slipped from Max's hands and flew into the bushes. Max went to retrieve it but stopped halfway when something caught his eye.

"What's that?" he asked, pointing at a nearby tree.

Morgan and Marshall followed his gaze and saw it, too. Something was sticking out of a hole in the middle of the tree.

Max walked over to get a better look. It was a rolled-up piece of paper dangling halfway out. He stood on his tiptoes and pulled it out.

He unrolled the paper and pressed it flat against a nearby rock. Morgan and Marshall gathered around to have a look.

"It looks like a treasure map," said Marshall with a twinge of excitement.

Max couldn't help but be doubtful. Who would hide a treasure map in boring old Whitebush? The paper was stained brown from the mud, and one of the corners had been ripped off.

"Treasure would be nice," agreed Max, "but I doubt it." He traced his finger along a dotted line to the missing corner.

Morgan leaned in. "Whoever made this map drew tons of trees over here. I think that's supposed to be the woods, isn't it?"

"Probably," nodded Marshall. "This winding line below the woods could be a road, or maybe a river."

"It has to be a river, there's a bridge drawn right there and even some cool drawings of fish," said Max.

"I agree," said Morgan. "And this open area looks to be a field of some kind." He looked more closely at it. "Wait a minute. It's a football field and it's the same one we just came from! See the parking lot and the playground? It's all the same."

"So, it's without question a map of Whitebush," Max said. "But why would anybody draw a map of Whitebush? Unless..." he paused.

Marshall's eyes lit up. "Unless it's a map to hidden treasure!"

"Don't get your hopes up. It could be a map to anything," said Morgan.

"Like what?" asked Marshall.

Morgan looked amused by the question. "The possibilities are endless. It could be a map to an underground bunker or even a dragon's lair."

Max cut in. "I thought dragons lived in caves on the sides of mountains."

"Maybe it's a cave without the mountain. Maybe the dragon is afraid of heights," replied Marshall.

Max smiled. "Let's not get too far ahead of ourselves. First, we must find out where the trail on the map begins, and more importantly, where it ends."

Max rolled the map up and stuffed it into his pocket. "We better get going back. Not a peep to anyone about this. Got it?"

He glanced at his watch. It was 5:30 pm. Dinner was in half an hour!

Dogs

Never approach a dog without getting permission from the owner. If the owner says no, it's for a good reason! The dog might be shy or not good around kids, or just plain mean like Lorenzo Duke! You could get a bite to your hand, and trust me, you don't want to go to the hospital to get stitches. Ouch!

If the owner does give permission, let the dog sniff your hand to get your scent before you pet it.

The Plan

After dinner, Max brought the map out and placed it on the table.

"Guess what?" he announced to his parents. "We found something in the woods."

"Whatever that something is, looks like it belongs in a trash can, not on my white linen tablecloth," Mrs. Walker declared.

Max blushed. "Sorry, Mom." He picked up the map and placed it on top of a chair instead. "We think it might be a treasure map."

"And that the loot is hidden somewhere in Whitebush," Marshall blurted.

Mr. Walker stood up and walked around the table, to have a closer look.

Max ran his finger down the map. "I think the path starts here, at the playing field, and then runs through the woods, down a hill, and over a footbridge, where it ends here," he pointed.

Mr. Walker looked confused. "Where's the rest of it?"

Max shook his head. "That's our problem. The corner of the map is missing. It looks like somebody ripped it off."

"And it's likely the spot where you hope you'll find the treasure," guessed Mr. Walker.

"Exactly," Max responded.

"Have you ever been down there before?" Morgan asked.

Mr. Walker laughed. "When I was a kid, my friends and I pretty much lived down there during the summer, camping and fishing and just having fun."

He pointed his finger at the footbridge. "This looks to be an old map. The bridge hasn't been there since 1985."

"What happened to it?" asked Morgan.

"That year, a major flood knocked the bridge over. It was a shame because after that, we no longer had a way across unless you were brave enough or dumb enough to try to swim it."

"What was on the other side?" asked Morgan.

"Some forests and meadows, a handful of ponds, and a few caves."

Marshall's eyes lit up. "Caves, you say. Maybe the treasure is hidden in a cave."

Mr. Walker shrugged. "It's possible."

"Even if it's buried in a cave, we'll have a hard time finding it without the missing corner of the map," Morgan pointed out.

"You guys are the Walker Boys. If anybody can track down the hidden treasure, it's the three of you!" Mr. Walker reminded them.

The Walker Boys were as well known for their exploits in football and hockey as they were for their crazy adventures. This adventure looked to be promising.

There was no denying it. Adventure was part of their DNA, along with the usual mix of danger, crime, and mystery. Their last adventure had been a good one, and they were lucky enough to have escaped unharmed. Discovering the Shooting Star was the icing on the cake. It was a cool gadget that they hoped to use soon.

The boys got up and cleared the table, then went to the kitchen in search of dessert.

"Rinse off the dishes and leave them in the sink," Mrs. Walker reminded them.

"By any chance, are we having dessert tonight?" asked Morgan.

Mrs. Walker shook her head. "Not tonight. The only thing we have are popsicles in the freezer."

Morgan was first to open the freezer. He had a wicked sweet tooth and ate just about anything that had sugar in it. He even sprinkled sugar on his broccoli when nobody was looking.

Morgan held up three popsicles. "I got first dibs on the red one!"

"I got blue," said Max.

Marshall frowned. "Pink again."

Max giggled. "First come, first serve."

Once the popsicles were finished, they headed upstairs to Max's bedroom, where they studied the map and came up with a plan. That night, sleep hit them fast and hard. Visions of treasure danced in their heads as they dreamed of the big adventure waiting for them the next day.

Responsibility

Do you help clean up after dinner? If you don't, you're not doing your part! Show your parents how much help you can be around the house. Cleaning up the dinner table and doing some dishes is a great way to demonstrate this.

It's called being <u>responsible.</u> You are in control and in charge of yourself and your own actions.

Are you responsible for doing your homework?

You bet!

Are you responsible for keeping a tidy room?

You bet!

Are you responsible for helping around the kitchen or dining room after meals?

You bet!

With more responsibility comes more freedom!

The Adventure Begins

I t was the following morning, and the Walker Boys were on their way to the football field. Their friend Jerry was going to meet them there. After he found out about the treasure map, he had to go, and he wouldn't take no for an answer. When they got to the field, Jerry was already there waiting for them.

"Arrr, mateys. Let's go find us some treasure!"

Max laughed and pulled out the map. He laid it flat on a picnic table.

The boys huddled around to have a look.

Max ran his finger down the map. "Looks like the trail is here," he pointed. "That's where we need to go."

"And where does the trail end?" asked Jerry.

"We don't know. The missing corner of the map is where the answer lies."

"And where is the missing corner?" asked Jerry.

Max rolled his eyes. "It could be anywhere. It'd be like trying to find your pet fish in the ocean."

"That would be nearly impossible," Jerry conceded, "but there's always a chance. Never say never."

Max folded the map up and waved them on. "Let's go find us some treasure."

They were soon in the woods walking along a winding dirt path. Max pushed aside a branch and squeezed past two pine trees.

"Watch out for the swinging branch!" he shouted as he let go.

"Ouch!" yelped Morgan. "That got me right in the face."

"Sorry," Max replied, trying hard not to laugh.

They lumbered on, skipping over a dead tree trunk, snaking through a web of vines, and climbing over a large moss-covered rock until they stumbled into a clearing.

Max pointed towards the far end of the clearing. Beside it sat a farmer's field enclosed by an old wooden fence. "It looks like the trail continues over there," he said.

They made their way over but didn't get very far before Jerry stumbled across something rather unpleasant.

"Oh, man!" yelped Jerry. "I just stepped in cow poop. I can't get my shoe out!"

Max grinned. "Looks like some of the cows must have gotten out."

Marshall laughed, "Looks like your white shoes have turned brown."

Max reached out and grabbed Jerry's hand to pull him free. With a sharp tug, the shoe plopped out.

"At least your brown shirt matches your brown shoes now," observed Morgan.

Jerry said nothing.

"Shhh, do you hear that?" Morgan whispered. "It sounds like there are people close by... and they're muttering something not nice."

All four tiptoed across the clearing to the edge of the woods.

Max gently pushed aside some branches. He saw two teenage boys hanging out. They looked like they were up to no good and did not want to be disturbed. One of them was built like a tank and had an uncanny resemblance to Lorenzo Duke. The other was skinny with hair that could have been used as a mop.

Max carefully let the branches slide back into place. "Those guys look tough."

Morgan ran through their options. "They're right in the middle of our trail. We could hide and wait for them to leave or try to get around them without being seen."

Jerry went to speak and opened his mouth halfway when he felt a sneeze coming on. "I, I think I'm going to sneeze. Ah, ah, ah... *achooo!* Drats!"

"Hey! Who's there?" a voice yelled.

Seconds later, the two teenage boys sprang out of the woods.

"What do you think you're doing?" the Tank said. "Were you spying on us?"

Max tried to be polite. "No, we're not spying on you. We're just walking on the trail, and you happen to be on it."

"Nobody comes out here except us! Not you brats. This is our land!" Jerry cut in. "I don't see a sign anywhere that says this is your land. I saw a sign further back, but it said something completely different."

The skinny one fell for it. "Oh, yeah, what did it say?"

"It said, 'Only Meatheads May Pass By.' We should have listened because we're not the meatheads, you guys are."

Morgan rolled his eyes. *Great*, he thought, *now we're in for it.*

The Tank lunged at Jerry and grabbed him by the collar, lifting him up so the two were at eye level. His face turned red.

"What did you say to me, punk?"

Jerry showed no sign that he was scared. "Yup, you're definitely a meathead, you can't even remember what I just said."

The Tank swung a wild left hook aimed squarely at Jerry's chin, but missed when Morgan came to the rescue, tackling him to the ground.

The stunned teenager pushed himself off the ground and turned to face Morgan.

Morgan, the peacekeeper, who used his words and brains more than his fists, had just done the unthinkable: he stood up to one mean bully.

Max stepped in the middle before the Tank could get to Morgan. At the same time, Marshall snuck behind the teenagers without being noticed.

"We don't want any trouble," Max said.

"Well, trouble just came, and it's going to lay a beat down," growled the Tank.

Max tried to buy some time. "I apologize for my brother. He's got Restless Arms Syndrome."

Both teenagers gave him a blank look. "There isn't such a thing. You're just making that up."

"No, it's the truth. Sometimes his arms have a mind of their own and just take over."

Max tried hard not to look at Marshall, who was crouched behind the two teenagers, tying their shoelaces together. When he tied the last knot, he gave them a thumbs up.

Max let out a sigh of relief. Now he could say whatever he wanted. "On second thought, I don't think he has Restless Arms Syndrome. He meant to tackle you because you guys had it coming."

If Max didn't know any better, he could swear he saw steam coming out of their ears. In a blink of an eye, the mean teenagers lunged at Max, but got tripped up when their feet didn't move, sending them headfirst into a big pile of cow poop!

Their faces were covered in it—it was in their noses, their ears, and their mouths.

With a look of satisfaction, the boys took off into the woods. They could hear the two mean teenagers howling and spluttering in disgust.

More on Bullies

Is it a good idea to throw insults at a bully? No!

This will only add fuel to the fire. The bonfire just became a raging inferno! Be assertive if you are confronted, but don't throw around insults. You'll be stooping down to the bully's level. Instead, rise above it. Say what you mean and mean what you say with confidence. Believe in yourself and stick to your guns! When your back is against the wall, you have nowhere to go but forward!

The Narrow Escape

Max could hear Jerry gasping for air behind him as they raced through the woods.

Morgan jumped over a fallen tree, trying hard not to trip. "Do you hear them? Are they chasing us?"

"I tied their shoelaces together in triple knots," huffed Marshall. "It'll be a while before they get them undone."

"And get themselves cleaned up," snickered Jerry.

Sensing they were no longer in danger, they stopped running and began to walk.

"That was close! *Too* close!" exclaimed Morgan.

"They sure were mad," said Max.

Marshall laughed. "Can you blame them? Who wouldn't be mad after diving headfirst into a pile of cow poop?"

"I thought getting my shoes covered in the stuff was bad enough," said Jerry.

They followed the trail down a long hill to the bottom, where they came to a river.

Max examined the river. "It sure looks bigger than the one on the map."

"And faster," confessed Morgan.

They hiked along the riverbank until they found what they were looking for. It was the bridge—or what was left of it.

Jerry looked confused. "Without a bridge there, how do we get across?"

Morgan studied the river. "We can't swim across, that's for sure. The current will sweep us away, and as our dad pointed out, it would be pure stupidity."

"Let's see if we can find a place to cross further up," Max said.

"Good idea!" agreed Marshall. Let's keep a lookout for it."

"And don't forget to keep a lookout for those mean teenagers," reminded Morgan. "I sure hope we don't run into them again."

They fought their way through a mesh of trees and shrubs—a mix of vines and plants so thick that it seemed to swallow them up like bugs in the grass. They didn't find a place to cross, but they did find the next best thing.

"Is that what I think it is?" blurted Marshall.

"That's a boat, all right, and it's our ticket to get across!" answered Max.

The boys walked over to examine it. It was a rowboat, and it looked old enough to be in a museum. Speckled flakes of blue and white paint peeled off its wooden exterior like a cracked eggshell.

"Do you think it's safe enough to use?" asked Morgan.

Jerry bent over to take a closer look. "I don't see any holes in it, just a lot of dents and scrapes."

He looked inside and frowned. "I don't see any oars or lifejackets, either."

"They must be hidden somewhere close by," said Max.

"What makes you so sure?" asked Jerry.

"Because somebody just used this boat, maybe a day ago."

"How do you know?"

"There's no water in the boat, and the last rainfall we had was two nights ago. We should see water pooled at the bottom, but there isn't any. Whoever used the boat emptied it of water."

"Unless there really is a hole in the boat," laughed Jerry.

After a quick search of the area, they found a single lifejacket and oars, hidden underneath the branches of a pine tree.

Marshall pulled them out. "We only have one lifejacket, but we'll need another three. Should we take a chance and go without them?"

Max shook his head. "If the boat sinks, we'll be in trouble. The undertow and the current could pull us under."

Morgan agreed. "Safety comes first. You should never go in a boat without a lifejacket."

Marshall said, "We have lifejackets at home. Why don't we go back and grab them?"

"Good idea," said Jerry.

The boys made their way back but didn't get far when trouble came knocking.

Boat Safety

Never, ever go into a boat without wearing a lifejacket! Drownings occur every year for just this reason. Just because you can swim doesn't mean you shouldn't wear a lifejacket.

Boaters sometimes have a false sense of security from being on a buoyant floating object (the boat). But what happens if you get thrown off the boat? It's you and the water, and the only thing keeping you up is your ability to swim.

Good swimmer, you say? What happens if your boat floats away and you're in the middle of a lake? What's going to keep you up then?

A lifejacket!

Baxter to the Rescue

Marshall was the first to spot them. It was Lorenzo Duke and the two mean teenagers.

Lorenzo stared at Max with an evil grin. "I told you I'd come back for you to finish the tackle. You and your nerdy brothers and that tall, gangly freak."

Max glared back at him. "I thought you meant on the football field, not off it."

"Well, you're wrong," Lorenzo grunted. He nodded at the Tank beside him, who rested a metal baseball bat over his shoulder.

"When my older brother told me what happened, I knew I had to help. Revenge is my middle name," grinned Lorenzo.

"I can see the resemblance," said Jerry. "Both your faces look like they got run over by a herd of wild goats."

Morgan shook his head and muttered under his breath. "Jerry and his big mouth."

Lorenzo's brother brought the bat down and clenched it with both hands. "You'll pay for that. Say hello to my little friend.

They call him Slugger, and he should be used for baseball, but I like to use him for other purposes."

The skinny teenager laughed, and Lorenzo smirked.

Jerry wasn't having any of it. "You guys look like you cleaned yourselves up. I don't see any cow poop on you, but I can sure smell it. Or is that just how you usually smell?"

"You just couldn't keep your mouth shut, could you, Jerry?" whispered Morgan.

Rage boiled over the two mean teenagers as they made a move towards them. Lorenzo stood back to watch the unfolding drama with a goofy grin on his face.

Lorenzo's brother was only a couple of steps away when something stopped him. A blur of black and white jumped out of the bushes and knocked him to the ground.

Shaken and confused, Lorenzo's brother looked up and saw his assailant. It was an animal—a dog, in fact. It was Mr. Barber's dog, Baxter, and he was off his leash again!

The lovable and fun-spirited Baxter seemed to sense danger. A deep rumbling growl, followed by a flash of white fangs, got Lorenzo's brother's attention. There was now no sign of Lorenzo or the other teenager. They had taken off in a hurry!

Lorenzo's brother looked petrified. "Get him away from me!" he begged.

Jerry put him in check. "Sorry, we can't do that. He's not our dog. But he sure is a good judge of bad character!"

Lorenzo's brother's eyes widened with fear. In a blink of an eye, he got to his feet and ran to the closest tree, where he leaped up the side and grabbed onto the nearest branch. Before he could pull himself up to safety, Baxter jumped up and bit him on the bum, pulling his pants clean off!

Ouch!" he screamed. "That dog just bit my bum!"

Max dug into his backpack and pulled out an instant camera. "Say cheese!"

A second later, the photo slid out, and Max held it up to show him. Lorenzo's brother blushed. "Give me that photo right now!"

"No can do," said Max, "but we'll leave your clothes behind. If you cause us any more trouble, we'll send this photo to your school's yearbook. It would look nice in there, wouldn't you say?"

Lorenzo's brother nodded his head sheepishly, "Okay, okay, you win! Just don't send that photo to the yearbook."

Max was only bluffing, but it worked.

"You got yourself a deal," said Max.

Jerry tossed the shredded clothes on the ground, and the boys walked on, each grinning from ear to ear.

"We better go find Mr. Barber. He'll be looking for Baxter," Morgan said.

Marshall chuckled, "It's a good thing Baxter got off his leash. I hate to think about what would have happened if he didn't."

"We wouldn't be smiling, that's for sure," answered Marshall.

"And wouldn't be alive to talk about it either," added Jerry.

"Baxter! Baxter, where are you, boy?" a voice shouted.

They saw Mr. Barber round a bend in the trail. "There you are, Baxter! He must really like you boys. Thank you for finding him—again."

"It's our pleasure," replied Morgan. "Let's just say that this time, we're the ones who owe you and Baxter a big thank you."

Mr. Barber shot him a quizzical look. "What exactly for?"

"Let's just say he arrived at the right place at the right time," said Morgan.

Mr. Barber still looked puzzled but decided not to ask any more questions, as the boys looked exhausted and a little shaken up. "Well, you're welcome," he said, putting the leash back on Baxter. With a wink and a wave goodbye, Baxter dragged him away.

When the boys got home, they agreed that they would come back the next day to finish what they had started.

That night, before tucking himself into bed, Max took out the Shooting Star and examined it. Nobody knew about it except for the three of them—not even their parents. During their last adventure, they had stumbled upon it by accident. He had a feeling that they were going to need it very soon.

Social Media

Mobile devices are everywhere. Videos and pictures are taken all the time. Just make sure that if somebody takes a photo or video of you, it's appropriate and even your grandmother would approve of it! If she wouldn't approve of it, don't have the picture taken!

Where do some of these pictures go? Social media: places like Snapchat, Instagram, and Facebook, just to name a few, and once they're up, they're tough to take down.

Bullies not only appear in person like Lorenzo Duke, but also behind a computer screen or a mobile device of some kind. Spreading rumors, using threats, and posting inappropriate pictures are all considered forms of bullying. If you or anyone you know is a victim of online bullying, tell an adult and get help!

The Rowboat

Max pointed at the floorboards of the boat. "Is that a Chocolate Puff wrapper?"

"Too bad there's nothing inside," replied Morgan. "My mouth is watering at the sight of it."

Chocolate Puffs were balls of chocolate filled with cream—a favorite candy of most kids in Whitebush.

It was the following morning. The boys were huddled around the boat. Their feet were soaking wet. Their shoes had soaked up the early morning dew like sponges as they stood in the knee-high grass.

"I don't recall the wrapper being there yesterday," said Morgan.

"Which means somebody must have used the boat after we left," answered Max.

"But who and why?" asked Marshall.

"I don't know, but we better watch our backs," cautioned Jerry. "Whoever it was could still be close by, maybe even watching us right now."

The boys looked around, suddenly aware of their surroundings.

"Catch." Max tossed out the lifejackets.

They put them on and climbed into the boat. Jerry inserted the oars as Marshall and Max pushed the boat onto the river and jumped aboard.

They were off! Jerry rowed hard as the boat plodded across the river, fighting the strong current until they reached the opposite shoreline.

They pulled the boat ashore and got out leaving their lifejackets behind. They made their way past a clearing peppered with rocks and covered in weeds and low-lying bushes. They stopped when they came to a sign that read, 'Keep Out, Dogs on Patrol.'

Morgan looked concerned. "Do you think we should go any further? The sign says to keep out. Maybe we should turn back."

Max shook his head. "Whoever put this sign up is trying to hide something."

"Like treasure!" exclaimed Marshall.

Max walked on.

"I guess that means we're not turning back," whispered Morgan.

They scooted around a swampy area and fought their way through a maze of towering cattails, until they reached a meadow sprinkled with flowers and surrounded by a lush green forest oozing the smell of fresh pine.

They stopped at the edge of the forest.

Max rechecked the map. "It looks like this is where the trail ends thanks to the missing corner. We'll have to look for..."

SNAP!

"What was that?" whispered Morgan.

"It sounds like a twig, or a branch just snapped," said Max.

"I think somebody is following us," hissed Jerry.

The boys stood still and listened but didn't hear anything except the chatter of birds.

Max waved them on, "It's probably nothing, just a small animal or something."

Jerry smiled. "Like a cute chipmunk."

They walked a little further but stopped didn't when they heard the same noise again. This time, it was much closer.

The boys spun around, and their eyes grew as large as two white saucers when they saw what had made the sound!

Maps

Most maps, just like the treasure map, have a compass rose. This shows the direction in which you'll be heading. North? East? South? West?

An excellent way to remember these directions is a simple phrase:

Never Eat Shredded Wheat.

The sun rises in the east and sets in the west, and around midday, it should be directly above you. In the morning, when you're walking toward the sun, which way are you headed?

East.

If you're walking in the exact opposite direction, which way are you headed?

West.

CAMPING & ADVENTURE

Did You Say Bear?

ear!" yelled Morgan

"Run!" yelled Max.

It was a bear! And it was charging right at them!

The boys ran for their lives, zigzagging around trees, leaping over rocks, and bulldozing their way through bushes and swinging branches.

"Find a tree to climb!" Max hollered. "It's our only chance!"

A couple of yards ahead stood a solid oak tree.

The boys dashed to the tree and climbed up before the bear arrived a few seconds later.

They huddled near the top of the tree, clinging on for dear life.

"Uh, guys?" said Morgan. "You do know that bears are good climbers, right?"

At that moment, the bear started to climb the tree.

Morgan checked his pockets. "Anybody have any food on them? Maybe he'll prefer that over us."

"I got nothing," said Max.

"I have a chocolate bar," said Marshall, "but I don't want to give it up."

Morgan glared at him. "Are you serious?"

The bear was so close now that the boys could smell its hot, rancid breath as it flashed its teeth in an angry snarl, foam spewing from the corners of it's mouth like an erupting volcano.

"Okay," Marshall sighed. He tossed the chocolate bar down.

The bear's attention shifted from the boys to the chocolate bar. It climbed back down the tree to investigate.

"Do we have any more food?" asked Morgan. "I don't think he'll be satisfied with just a chocolate bar. Hey, Jerry, what about you?"

Silence.

"Where's Jerry?"

Marshall shrugged. "Beats me."

"Me, too," said Max.

They looked around for Jerry but didn't see him. The bear seemed focused on the chocolate bar. In one bite, it was gone, and seconds later, so was the bear, disappearing deeper into the woods.

"I guess my chocolate bar isn't just satisfying but filling," said Marshall.

The boys crawled down the tree and split up to look for Jerry. They were immediately rewarded for their effort. Morgan found him. He didn't see him, but he sure felt him when he landed right on top of him!

Bears

You are not safe from a bear if you climb a tree! Bears are great climbers. Nor are you safe if you go in the water, as they're also excellent swimmers.

Black bears and brown bears tend to be shy and usually stay away from humans. If you encounter one, stop and remain calm. Slowly back away. Don't run, climb, or swim! If it's charging at you, look big, wave your arms around like a madman, and make a lot of noise! Only run away as a last resort!

The Cave

Morgan had fallen through a hole. He lay on top of Jerry in a crumpled heap.

Morgan rolled off. "That's one way to find you. Sorry I had to land in unannounced."

Jerry sat up and scowled. "Lucky for you, my body makes a good mattress. I only had the hard rock to fall on."

Morgan shouted up at the others, "I found him!"

Max and Marshall ran over, surprised to find Morgan at the bottom of a deep hole. Sitting beside him, dazed, and confused, was Jerry.

"You guys okay?" shouted Marshall.

Morgan shouted back, "I think so."

Max dropped a flashlight down the hole. "Tell me what you see."

Morgan caught it. He swept the beam of light around the inside. They were surrounded by flat rock walls which narrowed into a tunnel at the far end.

Marshall leaned closer to the hole. "What do you see?"

"Looks like a cave!" Morgan yelled back. "Come see for yourselves!"

Max took a rope from his backpack and wrapped it around a tree, then let the other end drop to the bottom of the hole. "We're coming down!"

When they reached the bottom, they saw Morgan and Jerry covered from head to toe in dust.

Jerry pointed down the cave. "That looks to be the only way to go."

They made their way through the cave, following the bobbing beam of the flashlight around turns and bends and over fallen rock, and through narrow sections they had to squeeze through to get past.

Eeetch!

"What was that?" panicked Jerry.

"It sounded like it came from above us," said Marshall.

Max shone the flashlight upward, and his heart went into his throat when he saw a dozen glowing eyes staring back at him. "Bats!" he screamed.

A flutter of wings and a whoosh of air whizzed past them as the boys dove for cover.

"Owwwww!" Jerry screamed. "There's a bat in my hair!"

He got to his feet and jumped around like a wild man, clutching and swatting at his hair until the bat fluttered away.

Marshall laughed. "Do you plan on trying out for the dance team? You do one mean bunny hop!"

"Really funny!" Jerry said. "It's all fun and games until you get a bat in your hair."

Max waved at them to follow. "Come on, you two, knock it off!"

A little further up, the cave came to a dead end.

"Looks like we're going to have to turn around. The only way out is the way we came in," Max said.

"Or is it?" questioned Morgan. "Shouldn't the air around us be still? I feel a slight breeze, which means…"

Marshall finished his thought. "There should be another exit. The cave must continue on somewhere else."

"But where?" asked Jerry.

91

"I don't see a way out, but I do see another Chocolate Puff wrapper," said Max, waving it above his head.

"Can I see it?" asked Marshall.

Max handed it over. Marshall peeled the wrapper back and smelled it.

"It smells fresh," he said.

"What are you, the Chocolate Puff police?" laughed Jerry.

"So, if it's fresh, whoever ate it was just down here," Max said, stating the obvious.

"And it's likely the same person who left the Chocolate Puff wrapper in the boat," concluded Morgan.

Max looked confused. "Why would this person hike all the way to the end of a cave just to eat a Chocolate Puff? It makes no sense."

Jerry leaned against the cave wall. "Maybe he likes to eat alone."

The wall suddenly moved. Jerry just about jumped out of his own skin! He had accidentally pushed a secret lever, causing the entire cave wall to open. All four boys' jaws dropped at the sight before them. Nobody said a word.

JESS WALKER

Caves

Never go into a cave without permission from an adult. Many dangers lurk inside caves, such as bats, bears, collapsing walls, lack of oxygen, and hidden holes, just to name a few! Every year countless youth find themselves lost or stranded in a cave. Some never return.

The Discovery

They stood in a massive cavern. It was packed with wooden boxes, lined up in rows and stacked one on top of the other all the way to the ceiling. Each box had the same label plastered on the side that read, 'Chocolate Puffs.'

Max pried open a lid from a wooden box. "Looks like we found a lifetime supply of Chocolate Puffs."

Chocolate Puffs spilled out of the box like an overflowing bucket of water. He picked one up and read the information printed on the package. "That's funny. It says this it was made in 1985."

"That's the same year as the major flood," said Morgan.

"Your point being?" asked Jerry.

Morgan smiled. He was beginning to connect the dots.

"These boxes are from a cargo ship that transports all kinds of stuff, like food and clothes and electronics and cars…"

"And let me guess, Chocolate Puffs," answered Jerry.

"Correct. After our dad told us about the flood of 1985, I looked online and found something interesting. During the flood, a cargo ship sank off the coast of Porcupine Bay, just upstream of here."

Max smiled. "I think Morgan just solved where these boxes came from. They must have fallen overboard when the ship sank."

"And the flood must have carried these boxes here," added Morgan.

"So, we figured out what the treasure is and how it got here, but we've failed to solve who the person is that's kept this place a secret for so long," concluded Jerry.

Marshall kicked a rock. "And whoever it is, how has he or she been able to eat so many Chocolate Puffs without turning into one. I see plenty of empty boxes."

Max asked, "Aren't these Chocolate Puffs too old to eat anyway? 1985 was a long time ago."

"Believe it or not, Chocolate Puffs don't go bad," replied Morgan. "Something in the ingredients and the way they're packaged makes them last forever."

Jerry unwrapped a Chocolate Puff and popped it into his mouth. "In that case, I'll eat one right now."

Max, Morgan, and Marshall did the same.

"Who needs to bring a snack when you can go to an all-you-can-eat Chocolate Puff cave?" said Jerry, biting into his seventh.

"Wait a minute," said Marshall. "There *is* a place you can go to eat only Chocolate Puffs. It's not a cave, but it is a café."

"Oh, yeah. It's called Chocolate Puff Café, and it's just off the main road before you enter town," said Morgan.

"I think we've all been there before, haven't we?" asked Max.

"The last time I was there, I had the Chocolate Puff sundae," said Marshall.

"And I had the Chocolate Puff double-decker pepperoni sandwich," said Jerry.

"And how can you forget the Chocolate Puff noodle soup?" said Morgan.

"So, whoever owns that restaurant may be our suspect," concluded Max.

"I don't know his name, but I remember what he looks like," said Jerry. "He has a shaved head and only one arm. He looks mean, and from what I've heard, *is* mean. Rumor has it that he once made a kid pick up every one of the Chocolate Puff French fries he accidentally spilled on the floor."

"That's not so bad," said Marshall.

"No, it isn't—until he made him get down on his hands and knees and eat them up like a dog!"

Morgan looked grossed out. "That's not just mean, that's plain nasty."

"And it's going to get nasty in here if the bats decide to come back," Marshall reminded them. "Follow me, I think I may have found a way out."

A tiny sliver of sunlight poked through the cave wall at the far end. It grew bigger and brighter as they came closer, until they stood right in front of it. It was a way out! Marshall walked through and returned seconds later, drenched in water.

Jerry looked puzzled. "How can it be raining out there if it's so sunny?"

"It's not rain," replied Marshall.

"If it's not rain, what is it?" asked Jerry.

"Go see for yourself."

They walked out and were surprised to feel water rushing down on them.

They looked up and were surprised to see that they were standing underneath a huge waterfall. Max pointed at a rock ledge hugging the side of the waterfall. "That must be our way out," he said, waving them on.

Soon, they were standing outside, clear of the waterfall.

Jerry looked relieved. "It's a good thing we found another way out of the cave. Climbing up a rope and through a tiny hole in the ground isn't my jam."

Morgan's face suddenly turned pale.

"Are you okay?" asked Max. "You look like you just saw a ghost."

"It's not a ghost I'm worried about," stammered Morgan. "Look behind you!"

Bad People

If a bad person tries to take you away or is chasing you, what should you do?

Run as fast as you can and scream at the top of your lungs so everybody can hear you. The more noise you make, the more attention is put on the stranger, and the more likely they'll stop chasing you!

Should you talk to a stranger? Never, ever talk to a stranger!

Who is a stranger? Somebody you do not know.

If a stranger offers to give you a ride in his or her car, should you get in? No! Not even if that person says they know your mom and dad and that they gave permission to pick you up. You should have a secret password that only you and your parents know. If this stranger doesn't know the password, run like the wind!

If a stranger asked you to come into the woods to look for his lost dog, would you?

No! Bad people try to lure kids away from safety and other people. When they get their victim alone, bad things can happen.

These are scary what-ifs, but they happen every day, and something like this could happen to you if you don't practice good safety skills!

The Show-Down

It was a bald headed man, and he was running right at them! He had only one arm. It was the owner of the Chocolate Puff Café.

"Back to the cave!" shouted Max.

The boys scampered back into the cave.

"What now?" cried Jerry. "He's going to be here any minute!"

"Quick, hide!" shouted Max. "I think I have a plan that just might work."

"Does it involve the Shooting Star?" asked Marshall.

Max winked back, "You bet."

"Uhh, what's the Shooting Star?" asked Jerry.

"You'll find out soon enough," said Max.

Max hid behind a box near the entrance. He took out the Shooting Star from his backpack. The gold-plated device was no bigger than the palm of his hand and shaped like a chalk brush. A star-shaped object was attached to the end of it.

Seconds later, the one-armed man burst inside the cavern in an angry rage. "Are you kids in here? You better come out right now! If you don't, I'm going to hurt you!"

Max held his breath, trying not to make a sound. A flashlight beam bounced off the walls, bobbing up and down as the man walked closer and closer until he was within striking distance.

Now was his chance! Max jumped out of hiding and aimed the Shooting Star at the one-armed man's legs, squeezing the trigger. The star shot out like a cannonball, dragging a cord behind anchored by tiny metal weights. The instant it made contact, the cord wrapped around the man's legs several times until he was tied up. He fell to the ground with a thud.

Max came out from behind the box and was joined by Morgan, Marshall, and Jerry.

They walked over and stood around him.

The one-armed man rasped, "You better get me out of this or else…"

"Or else what?" asked Jerry. "You're going to come and get us? Looks like you're a little tied up at the moment."

That angered the one-armed man even more. He rolled toward Jerry and grabbed his ankles.

"I might not be able to use my legs, but I can sure use my one arm!" he shouted, pulling Jerry to the ground.

Marshall was thinking two steps ahead. He dashed over and jumped on the one-armed man's hand, coming down on it like a sledgehammer.

"Ouch!" The man jerked back in pain. "I think you just broke my one good hand!"

Max knew he had to get help before things turned ugly. "You guys stay here and guard him. I'm going to get help!"

He raced out of the cave and followed the trail back to the river—but when he got there, the boat was gone! He looked around but didn't see it anywhere.

"I might not be able to float across the river, but I could try to fly," he muttered.

He took out the Shooting Star and spun the dial until it read 'Grappling Hook'.

He spotted a tall pine tree on the other side of the river and took aim. He squeezed the trigger and the star shot out, dragging behind a cord that was still attached to the device. The star hit the tree and wrapped around it until the cord was pulled tight.

Max took a deep breath. "Here goes nothing!"

He pushed the trigger again and was shot out as the cord pulled him across the river. He zipped across to the other side, where he jumped off and landed on solid ground.

Before Max could get his bearings, the
bushes started to move. He immediately
thought of the mean teenagers and Lorenzo
Duke. Did they come back to get even with
him? He turned to run but stopped when he

heard a familiar sound. It was a bark and it belonged to Baxter the dog.

He saw Baxter emerge first, followed by Mr. Barber who was out of breath and breathing heavy.

"Sorry, Max, I don't know what's gotten into Baxter today. He dragged me down here, half whining and half growling the whole time. It's as though he sensed somebody was in danger."

Max nodded. "He was right."

He told Mr. Barber what had happened— about the mean teenagers, the bear, the cave, the bats, the Chocolate Puffs, and finally, the crazy one-armed man chasing them.

Mr. Barber shook his head in disbelief. "Your story is better than any action book I've ever read! I'm glad you're still around to talk about it."

He took out his phone and called the police. An hour later, Max, a policeman, Mr. Barber, and Baxter stood outside the waterfall.

Max waved at them to follow before he disappeared underneath it. The policeman and Mr. Barber looked puzzled but followed Anyway. When Max entered the cavern. He was relived to see that Jerry and his brothers were okay. The one armed man was still there, tied up and silent. "Why is he so quiet?" asked Max.

Marshall grinned and pointed at his own feet. "Notice anything different?"

"You only have one sock on," observed Max.

"Guess where the other sock is?"

Max looked down at the one-armed man and saw a dirty sock stuffed into his mouth.

"That's one way to keep him quiet."

"And I think the socks are so stinky, the smell might have knocked him out," laughed Jerry.

Officer Rodriguez walked over and shook the boys' hands with a big smile.

"You've done one heck of a job here today. I better be careful you don't take over my job," he laughed as he bent down and handcuffed the one-armed man. "Get home and get some rest. I have a lot of questions for you, but that can wait until tomorrow."

JESS WALKER

Emergencies

If there's an emergency, who should you
call? 911.

When you talk to the operator, try to remain calm.

Tell them your name, your location, and what the emergency is. They are there to help you, and the more information you provide, the easier their job will be.

Emergency Services consists of:

- ☑ Police
- ☑ Fire
- ☑ Ambulance

Case Closed

The next morning, there was a knock at the door. It was Officer Rodriguez. Morgan opened the door and led him into the kitchen, where Max, Morgan, Marshall, Jerry, and Mr. and Mrs. Walker sat around the table waiting.

"You should be very proud of these young men. What they did was remarkable," announced Officer Rodriguez.

Mr. Walker broke in. "And a little crazy and dangerous too. It's nothing new around here, though. This isn't their first adventure, nor will it be their last."

Officer Rodriguez turned serious. "The man you captured is Mr. Johnstone, the owner of Chocolate Puff Café. He's been in business since 1985. The stockpile of Chocolate Puffs you found is what he's been using to run his café illegally. After we got his fingerprints at the police station, we found out that he's wanted for other crimes, some of them much more serious. You're all lucky that nothing bad happened to you."

He opened a box and took out four shiny gold medals. "These are for you. They're Medals of Bravery.

Officer Rodriguez gave them a salute and a nod of approval before he walked out of the kitchen.

The boys sat in silence, admiring their medals.

"Even though we didn't find any pirate treasure, this has to be the next best thing," said Marshall.

"And don't forget the cool gadget we found inside one of the boxes," added Morgan.

Max raised his eyebrows. "What gadget?"

"When you went for help, we got hungry waiting. So, we opened a box to eat some more Chocolate Puffs but found something else inside—and boy, is it is ever cool!"

Jerry cut in. "More like out of this world and never-seen-before different!"

"What is it?" asked Max.

Marshall smiled. "You'll have to wait and see for our next adventure.

"Speaking of adventures, I have one for you right now," said Mrs. Walker.

"And what's that?" asked Max.

"It's to go upstairs and clean your bedrooms."

Jerry shot them a playful grin. "I guess that's my cue to leave. Happy cleaning, Walker Boys!"

A voice yelled at them from the hallway. It was Mr. Walker, and he sounded excited. "You guys need to come to the front door and see this!"

When they opened the door, they were surprised to see a lifetime supply of Chocolate Puffs!

THE END

About the Author

Born in 1974, Jess Walker is a Canadian author of children's and young adult literature. He writes fun, action-packed outdoor adventure stories mixed with the fundamental tenants of timeless life lessons aimed at building character, confidence, and safety awareness. He strives to inspire today's youth to get outside more (away from the screen) and make their own adventures happen.

More Books by This Author:

<u>Walker Boys Series</u>
Treasure Hunters

The Warrior Cup

Bigfoot

Like my book? Check me out on Facebook!

@ Author Jess Walker

Suggestions or comments.

Love to hear from you!!

<u>jesswalkerbooks@hotmail.com</u>

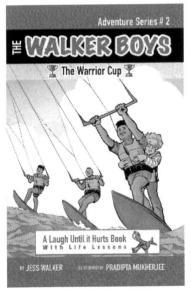

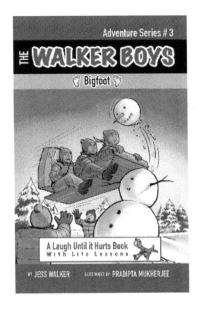